Dan McGinley's 4th grade picture from 1988

Dan McGinley lives with his wife and three children in South Jersey, where he teaches elementary school. He loves creating stories, poems, music, games and other miscellaneous ideas for others to enjoy.

To Miranda,

Never stop reading!

Dan McG

Aubrey Fitch lives in New Jersey with her husband, Sean and daughter, Lauren. She graduated from Rowan University and received her Bachelor's Degree in Art Education. This is her first attempt in illustration. She currently teaches art at an elementary school in South Jersey.

Aubrey Fitch

Thanks to Daniel, Chase, Addison and Justine for your love and support. Thanks to Jeanne, Angela and Raylene for your multiple edits and revisions. Thanks to Aubrey for making this book come to life with your amazing illustrations. And thanks to all those who have lent an ear to my countless crazy ideas over all these years! -D.M.

Thank you to Dan McGinley for the privilege of illustrating your wonderful book! These illustrations are dedicated to Jean (Gram) Finkbeiner. I promise to, one day, illustrate your writings. I love you. To my daughter Lauren, I hope you always want to read every book in the house before bed. To my parents who believe in doing what makes you HAPPY, not rich. (Though both would be nice!) And for Sean. You give me the confidence to create anything and everything. I love you. -A.F.

ISBN-13: 978-1491242698

ISBN-10: 1491242698

Written by Dan McGinley
Illustrated by Aubrey Fitch

Marisa was eating her breakfast one morning, When all of a sudden she heard a harsh warning.

The newscaster came
on the TV to say,
"The first case of Moo Flu
has popped up today."
Marisa was worried
becoming quite nervous,
Black and white spots
appeared with this virus.
"His skin's like a cow!"
is what someone had said,
After seeing the boy
while he lie there in bed.

The principal told Marisa's
teacher real quickly,
To tell the Moo Flu boy to
stay home while sickly.
Marisa was sad since that
boy was her friend,
So she volunteered to deliver
the work they would send.

She hoped to be able
to talk to her chappy,
To see how sad he may be
or how happy.
If she had this sickness
she may have a smile,
She liked the idea of
missing school for a while.

But when she arrived
 to visit the boy,
She found that this illness
would not bring her joy.
For as soon as the mom
saw Marisa arrive,
She said she could not
take one step inside.
So Marisa handed over
 the school work and turned,
Walked away from his house
 with much *utter* concern.

She glanced one last look
up to the boy's room,
A white and black hand
was all that did loom.

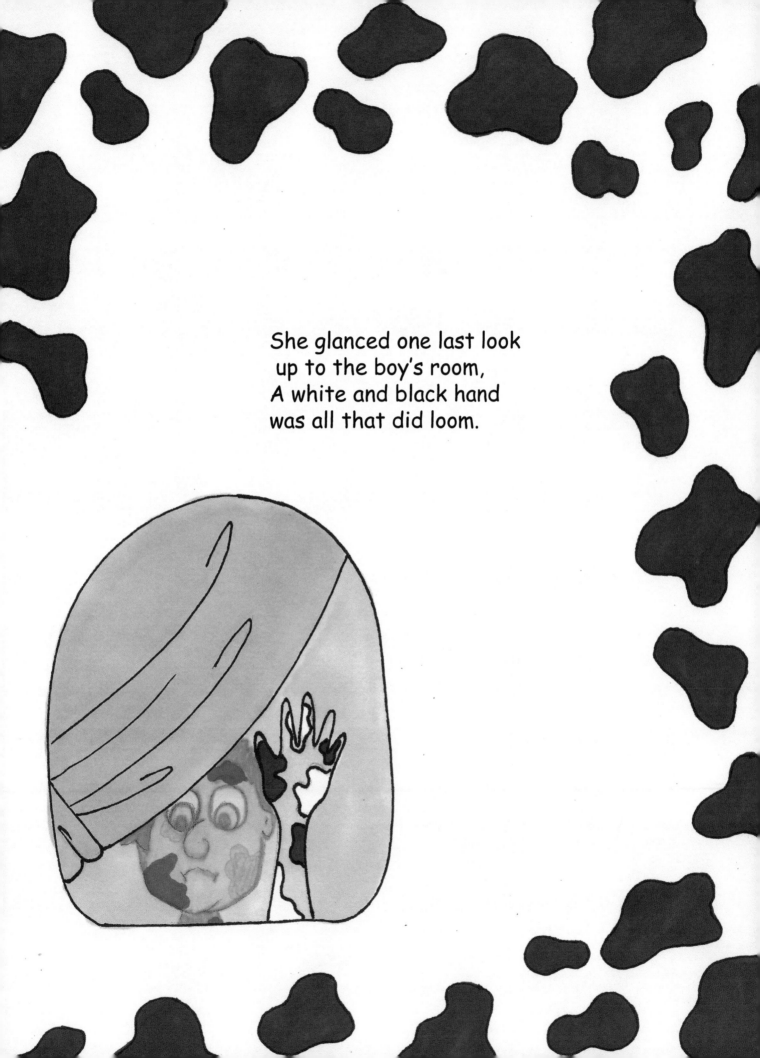

Back home, Marisa told
her Mother the news,
Who said the boy's friendship
is one she must lose.
"Just by looking at him,"
her mom squeamishly said,
"The Moo Flu will end up
right up on your head!"

Marisa did not want to
believe her own mother,
But knew she said it
because she did love her.
The next day in school
the word had got out,
Kids and teachers
were spreading rumors about.
The Moo Flu will get you
if you just breathe,
Or walk or talk
or even look at this disease.

So the school board convened and issued an order,
The boy was not welcome at school any longer.

Signs were put up
all over the town,
That made Marisa feel
dreary and down.
There were posters and writings
all over the walls,
Saying he was too dangerous
for even phone calls.

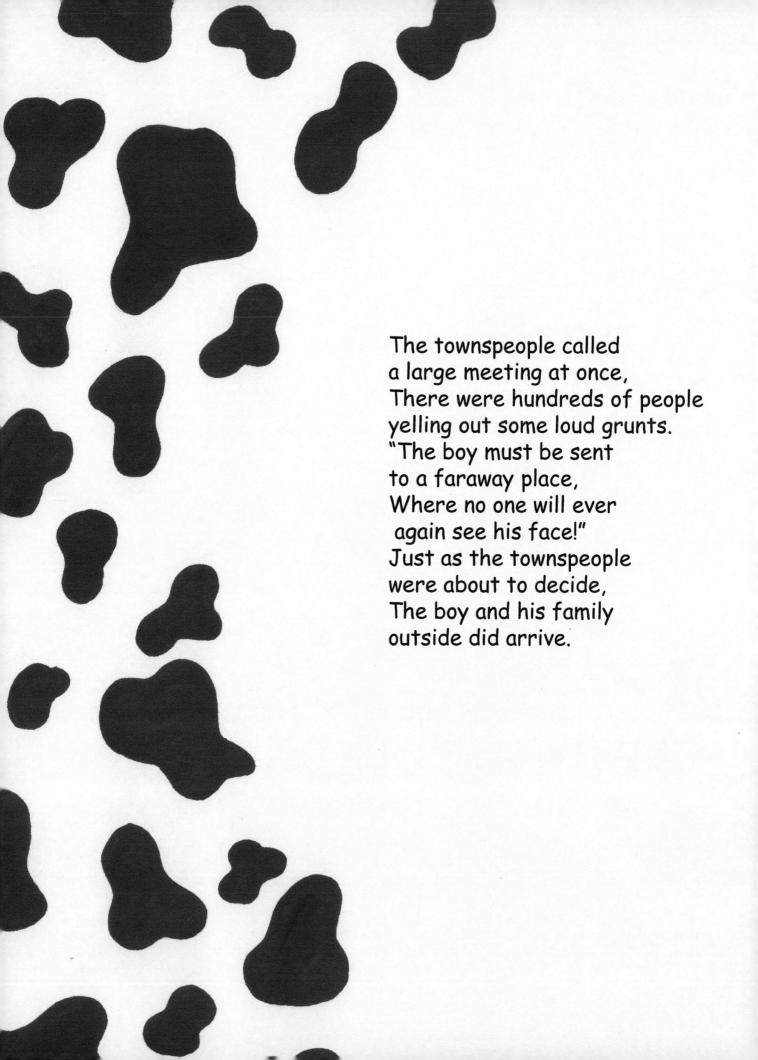

The townspeople called
a large meeting at once,
There were hundreds of people
yelling out some loud grunts.
"The boy must be sent
to a faraway place,
Where no one will ever
 again see his face!"
Just as the townspeople
were about to decide,
The boy and his family
outside did arrive.

They tried to get into
the meeting to say,
How the boy had become
to be looking this way.
The folks were scared
and would not let them in,
Then a sly idea made
Marisa's face show a grin.

She went to the bathroom
and when she came out,
The whole group exclaimed
and let out a shout.
They pointed and backed
all the way to the wall,
A black and white face
on Marisa they saw.

Marisa marched her way
right up to the door,
No one dared stand
in her way anymore.
She let in her friend
and another man too,
The man was her uncle,
Dr. Douglas Dagoo.
The Doctor stood up
to address the large crowd,
Telling all the results of
which he had found.
The truth of this sickness
they all dreadfully feared,
And how their reactions
were so very weird.

"A person cannot get
the Moo Flu so easy,
As being around someone
that may appear weezy.
The Moo Flu is one
of those types of sickness,
That's not contracted
just by being a witness.
There are certain rules
for how it can spread,
Not those silly things
all you people have said.
The boy is not someone
to treat disrespectful,
And pushing him out of the town
was just dreadful.
How would you like
to be treated this way?
It would make you feel
awful!" he started to say.

Then one man jumped up
to the front with a fright,
"Well, then how come Marisa
has turned Black and White?"

Marisa reached in her pocket
and pulled out a cloth,
Then rubbed those spots on
her face right clear off.
The townspeople's action
had her stomach in knots.
So she tricked all those people
by painting the spots,
Marisa devised this idea
and also had planned,
To call her uncle
to help them understand.

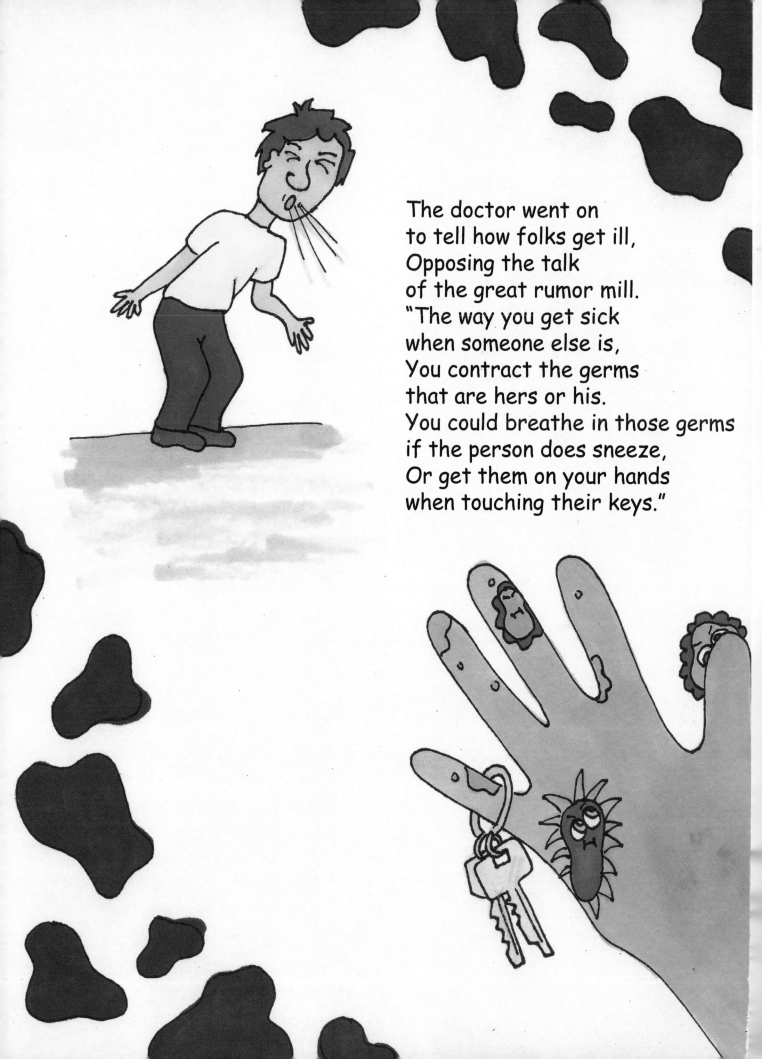

The doctor went on
to tell how folks get ill,
Opposing the talk
of the great rumor mill.
"The way you get sick
when someone else is,
You contract the germs
that are hers or his.
You could breathe in those germs
if the person does sneeze,
Or get them on your hands
when touching their keys."

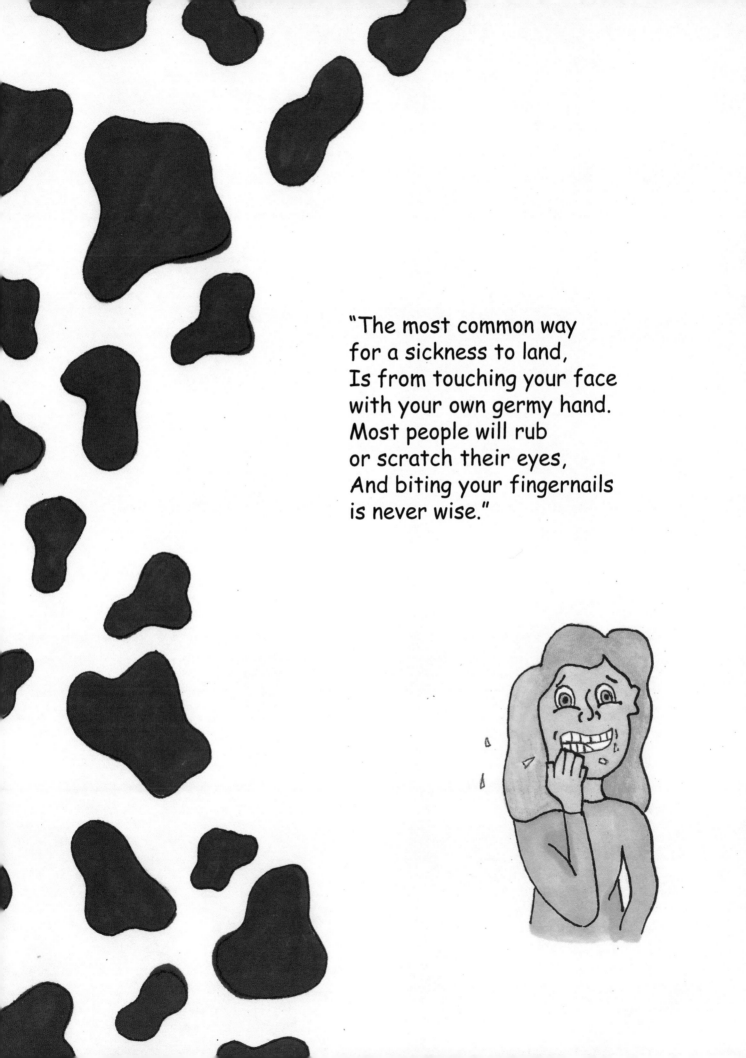

"The most common way
for a sickness to land,
Is from touching your face
with your own germy hand.
Most people will rub
or scratch their eyes,
And biting your fingernails
is never wise."

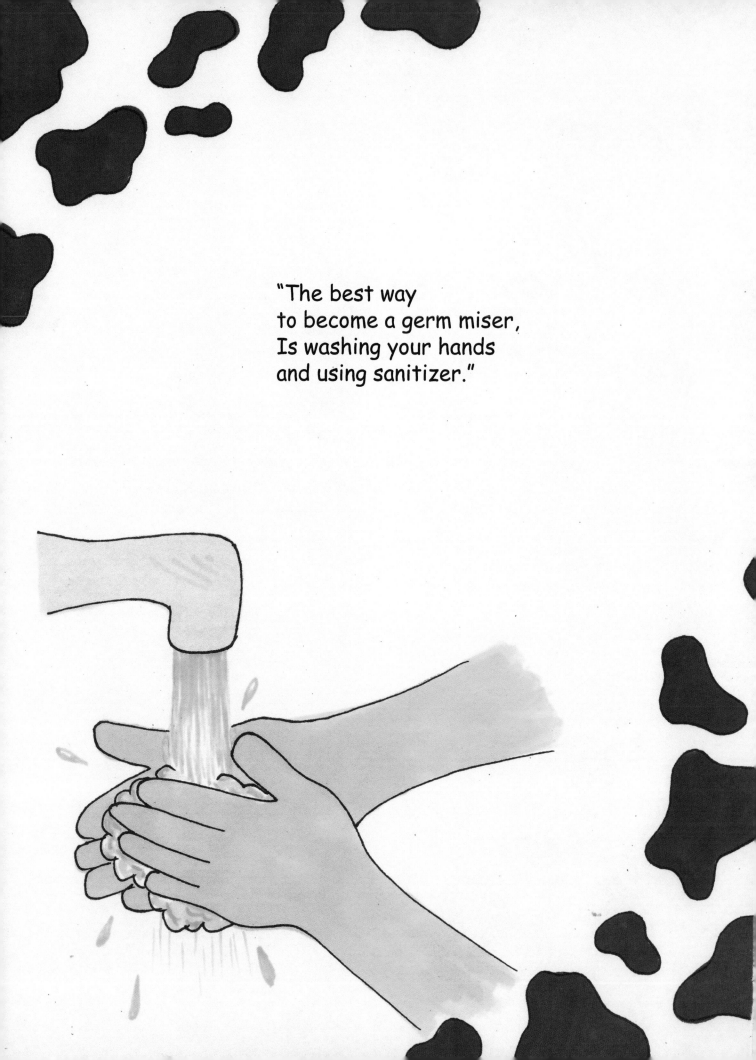

"The best way
to become a germ miser,
Is washing your hands
and using sanitizer."

"You all should have seen this
with a clearer iris.
Just hanging around him
cannot give you this virus."

Finally, the boy spoke up
to say it was lame,
To call him those things
for he has a name.
"My name is ROBERT,"
he yelled out so proud,
"Not Moo Flu or Cow Kid,"
he screamed to the crowd.
They all bowed their heads
as if taking the blame,
Treating Robert badly
had made them feel shame.

They said they were just
scared a little you see,
And worried about getting
the spots was the key.
But now that the Doctor
had taught them the truth,
They'd show more character
and respect this youth.
Then quiet as mice
no more words did they say,
Exited the door,
walked home straight away.
Robert turned around
to his very best friend,
And thanked her for all
the support she did lend.

So later that week
Robert returned to school,
The townspeople had thrown
out their silly new rule.
Marisa escorted her
friend to the door,
Hoping the kids would
bother Robert no more.

He still had remnants
left up on his face,
The black and white blotches
were faded in place.
As he opened the door
he was very relieved,
No one was there
to tell him to leave.
Not one single person
was even around,
What did it mean?
Had everyone left town?

Marisa grabbed his hand
and ushered him in,
All the teachers and children
were inside the gym.
A gigantic sign was
hanging from the ceiling,
The words gave Robert
a very good feeling.
"Welcome Back. We are sorry!"
in large ABCs,
What a shock beheld Robert,
and it wasn't a tease.
All of their faces had a
black and white patch,
They were painted the same
so that all of them match.

The group hoped their faces
might help him accept,
Them back in his heart
and forgive their neglect.
Robert smiled to show
he no longer felt blue,
Then made them all laugh
when he yelled out a, "MOO!"

A few weeks went by and
the Moo Flu had passed,
The black and white spots
 did no longer last.
Normal life returned
for the whole town,
Except for what Marisa
and Robert had found.

While walking to school
they saw on the street,
Their friend Michelle
had something near her feet.
She had a weird thing
obstructing her stance,
A flat waffle print tail
that was starting to dance.

Marisa and Robert hugged
their friend, didn't leave her.
They were not scared at all
of this dreaded Beaver Fever!

26163515R00020

Made in the USA
Charleston, SC
27 January 2014